HOW ARE YOU ?

FOR TOMORROW ...

NAZAR

Made with ♥ on the Notion Press Platform
www.notionpress.com

To The One and Only God Who Looks After Me.....

Contents

Foreword

In the depths of human experience lies a spectrum of emotions, from the brightest joys to the darkest sorrows. This book delves into the shadows of existence, exploring the complexities of life through the eyes of a character shaped by tragedy, loss, and a relentless search for meaning.

Preface

In these pages, you will encounter a narrative that transcends conventional storytelling. It is a journey through the depths of the human psyche, where emotions are both elusive and profound. Each chapter unveils layers of introspection, offering insights into the intricacies of survival, identity, and the consequences of our choices.

Prologue

In a world where emotions reign supreme, there exists a realm untouched by their tumultuous waves. It is a realm inhabited by a solitary figure, navigating the landscapes of existence with a detached curiosity. This is not a story of heroes and villains but a chronicle of a soul adrift in a sea of numbness and introspection.

ONE

The Interview

"I am fine, thank you.
How are you?
Why do you want to interview me?"
"Oh, I get it now.
I am different from you guys, aren't I?
So, you want to know about my life.
Well, where should I start?"

TWO

A Tragic Beginning

I was 12 years old when my parents passed away. They were shot right in front of me by a robber.

It was a beautiful day when my parents and I embarked on a trip to the beach. The sun was shining brightly, casting a golden glow on the sand and the waves. We laughed and played, enjoying the warmth of the sun and the cool breeze from the sea.

Little did I know that this seemingly perfect day would turn into a nightmare. As we were leaving the beach, a person appeared out of nowhere and confronted us. In a split second, everything changed. I watched in horror as the robber pointed a gun at my parents and demanded their belongings.

The tranquility of the beach was shattered by the sound of gunfire. The sound in my ear just became like a buzz, everything around me felt unrealistic. I stood frozen, unable to comprehend the sudden violence that had unfolded before me. The beauty of the day was eclipsed by the tragedy that befell us.

My parents fell to the ground, their lives taken away in an instant. The beach, once a place of joy and relaxation, became a scene of chaos and despair. I was left alone, a witness to the brutality of the world.

I don't know what to do. I was just standing there when people discovered it, they said I was a brave kid who just made it out alive. But as time passed, they started to say that I am a weirdo who doesn't feel anything. Guess they're right. I don't feel anything at all, what they used to call happy, sad, affection, etc. It's hard to live with these humans; I keep imitating others to survive."

The day my parents died is etched into my memory with painful clarity. The suddenness of their loss, the violence of their passing, it all happened in the blink of an eye. I stood frozen, unable to comprehend the magnitude of what had just occurred. People around me spoke in hushed tones, marveling at my apparent bravery for having survived such a traumatic event. Little did they know, it wasn't bravery that kept me standing—it was shock, numbness, and a profound sense of emptiness.

In the days and weeks that followed, I became a subject of fascination and scrutiny. People marveled at my ability to remain composed, to not shed a single tear for the loss of my parents. They called me a survivor, a resilient soul who had faced tragedy head-on and emerged unscathed. But inside, I was anything but unscathed.

THREE

SEARCHING FOR FEELING

As time passed, the initial shock gave way to a deep sense of emptiness that engulfed every corner of my being. I tried desperately to process the emotions that eluded me—happiness, sadness, affection—but they felt like distant memories, fleeting glimpses of a life I once knew. The vibrant colors of joy seemed muted, the weight of sorrow too heavy to bear, and the warmth of affection like a distant dream.

I watched others grieve, their tears and anguish a stark contrast to my stoic facade. Their words, though well-meaning, were like echoes in a cavernous void, reminding me of my perceived abnormality. I felt like an outsider, a puzzle piece that didn't fit into the intricate mosaic of human emotions and connections. Every smile I forced felt like a mask, every interaction a calculated performance to conceal the emptiness within.

My face became a mask of perpetual neutrality, betraying no hint of joy, sorrow, or anger. To others, I appeared serene, unaffected by the tumultuous currents of human feelings. My voice carried no inflections, devoid of the cadence that colors ordinary conversations. I navigated social interactions with mechanical precision, mimicking appropriate responses learned through observation rather than heartfelt understanding.

One day, amidst the chaos of my inner turmoil, I encountered a wise monk who saw through my facade. He looked into my eyes and spoke with a voice that resonated with wisdom and compassion. 'Your eyes hide a vast emptiness,' he said, 'a void that isolates you from the vibrant tapestry of human experiences. Yours is a paradox, present yet distant, a puzzle that others cannot unravel.'

His words echoed in the chambers of my soul, stirring emotions I thought were long buried. The emptiness inside me grew, a gaping void that no amount of pretending could fill. I longed to feel something, anything, but it seemed as though my emotions had shut down completely, leaving me adrift in a sea of numbness.

And so, I navigated through life with a heavy heart and an empty soul. The loss of my parents had left a void that nothing could fill, a void that defined my existence and shaped my interactions with the world. I was lost in a labyrinth of emotions I couldn't comprehend, adrift in a world that no longer felt like home.

FOUR

A Failed Relationship

After observing and analyzing potential partners, I finally found a girl who seemed suitable for my experiment. She was good-looking and average-educated, and her behavior intrigued me enough to pursue her. I spent weeks following her, studying her habits, likes, and dislikes, all in an attempt to understand her better.

Eventually, I decided it was time to make my move. I orchestrated a meeting at the library, a place where I felt comfortable and in control. I had her friend, whom I had befriended with treats and favors, bring her to the designated spot.

As she sat across from me, I mustered all the acting skills I had learned over the years. I put on a convincing show of affection, mimicking the behavior I had observed in others who were in love. With a blushing face that I had practiced in front of the mirror, I professed my love to her.

much to my astonishment, she responded in kind. She confessed that she had known me from before, as she used to be my junior. She admitted to having a crush on me back then but had never approached me because she thought I didn't like her.

However, what she didn't know was that I was always in the same emotionless state as everyone around me. I showed no particular interest or affection, which led her to believe that I didn't like her either. Despite her feelings and our brief previous conversation, I had forgotten about it entirely. My mind was focused solely on my experiment, on understanding the intricacies of love through observation and mimicry. The irony of the situation didn't escape me—she liked me, and I was conducting an experiment on love with her as the unwitting subject.

Our relationship began, and for a while, I played the part of a loving partner. However, as time passed, the facade became harder to maintain. Her constant calls, clingy behavior, and interruptions to my solitude started to wear on me.

I found her presence suffocating, her neediness a stark contrast to my desire for independence. I tried to endure it, but the charade became unbearable. I realized that I had used her as a means to an end, a way to fulfill my own curiosity about emotions I couldn't genuinely experience.

I laid bare the truth about my feelings—or rather, the lack thereof. I confessed the painful reality that I had been merely playing a role, a puppeteer manipulating strings in a desperate attempt to understand the elusive concept of love.

Her reaction was nothing short of devastating. The air crackled with an electric intensity as she absorbed my words, her eyes widening in disbelief and betrayal. The silence that followed was deafening, punctuated only by the echo of my confession ringing in my ears like a haunting melody of regret.

Tears welled in her eyes, mirroring the tempest raging within her soul. With a quivering voice choked by emotion, she pleaded for me to reconsider, to not abandon what we had built together. My determination was fueled by the harsh reality that I could no longer live a lie. I couldn't continue pretending to be someone I wasn't, just to appease societal expectations and norms. The weight of that realization bore down on me like a crushing weight, threatening to suffocate any remnants of the person I once thought I was.

Our final moments together were a whirlwind of tears, anguish, and unspoken words. She clung to me, her grip a desperate plea for me to stay, to rewrite the script of our love story. But I knew that rewriting the script would only perpetuate the façade, trapping us both in a cycle of deception and unfulfilled promises.

And so, I made the excruciating decision to sever all ties. I changed my contact information, a symbolic gesture of closing the chapter on a love that was never truly real.

Days turned into weeks, and The silence between us stretched like an endless abyss, a void filled with unanswered questions and unspoken regrets. I found solace in the quiet solitude of my own thoughts, grappling with the aftermath of a decision that had irrevocably altered the course of our lives.

But fate, it seemed, had other plans. Just when I thought the echoes of our shattered love had faded into obscurity, she reached out to me. Her voice trembled with emotion as she confessed her undying love, a love that transcended the boundaries of time and space.

Her words were like a siren's call, tempting me with the promise of redemption and reconciliation. Yet, I knew that answering that call would only reopen Herwounds, reopening wounds that had barely begun to heal.

And so, I stood at a crossroads, torn between the pull of the past and the uncertain promise of the future. Little did I know, my actions would set in motion a chain of events that would change the trajectory of our lives forever.

FIVE

CONSEQUENCES

After our breakup, she spiraled into deep despair and took her own life. The weight of her death hung heavy on my shoulders, knowing that I was the catalyst for her tragic end. Despite this knowledge, I resigned myself to the fate that awaited me.

The morning after her suicide, the police arrived at my doorstep, their expressions somber and accusing. I was taken into custody and transported to the courthouse, where the gravity of my actions began to sink in. I was charged with being the indirect cause of her death, a responsibility I couldn't deny.

In court, I faced the accusing stares of her grieving family and friends. Their anger and sorrow pierced through me, but I remained stoic, accepting my guilt without protest. I didn't try to defend myself or argue for leniency. In a way, I welcomed the punishment that awaited me, for it seemed fitting to bear the consequences of my actions.

When the verdict was announced, sentencing me to a term in prison, I accepted it with a sense of resignation. I was escorted to my cell, the heavy iron door closing behind me with a finality that mirrored the weight of my remorse.

In prison, a false accusation arose about me. It was said that I was imprisoned for killing six people in broad daylight. This accusation circulated among the inmates, shaping their perception of me. However, the truth is that both I and the actual perpetrator, who indeed committed the crime of killing six people on the same day, were arrested simultaneously. In a last-minute twist, he was transferred to another prison. Consequently, the inmates here mistook me for the perpetrator.

Despite knowing the misunderstanding, I chose not to correct it. Surprisingly, this false belief worked in my favor, as no one dared to confront or trouble me. It brought an unexpected peace amidst the challenging environment of prison life.

Prison life was stark and regimented, yet strangely comforting in its predictability. I found solace in the routine, the monotony of days passing by without the burden of pretending to feel emotions I no longer possessed.

Days turned into weeks, and weeks into months. I became accustomed to the confines of my cell, finding a strange sense of peace in the confines of my incarceration. I no longer had to navigate the complexities of human emotions or the expectations of society. Inside those walls, I was free from judgment, free from the facade of normalcy.

As time passed, I found a semblance of contentment within the confines of my confinement. The prison library became my sanctuary, offering a refuge from the harsh realities of the outside world. I immersed myself in books, finding solace in the worlds created by words and imagination.

I embraced my solitude, finding comfort in the absence of emotional entanglements. The guards became familiar faces, the routine of prison life a comforting rhythm that anchored me in a sea of uncertainty.

In the end, I realized that my imprisonment was not just a punishment but a sanctuary. A place where I could exist without the burden of pretending to feel, without the expectations of others weighing me down. Inside those walls, I found a strange sense of freedom, a freedom from the emptiness that had plagued me for so long.

And so, in the confines of my prison cell, I found a measure of peace. A peace born from acceptance, from facing the consequences of my actions, and from embracing the solitude that had become my refuge.

SIX

A Shadow in the Past

After my release from prison, the world outside felt like a stage set ablaze with chaotic emotions, a cacophony of feelings I could no longer comprehend. It was during this tumultuous time that I crossed paths with her brother, a tempest of rage and vengeance lurking beneath his façade.

Our meeting crackled with tension, words sharpened like daggers in a deadly dance of veiled threats and simmering animosity. In that charged moment, as the air thickened with the weight of unspoken histories and unresolved grievances, I remained an impassive observer, a marble statue untouched by the storm brewing around me.

When the storm finally erupted into violence, I acted with mechanical precision, a well-oiled machine executing a predetermined script of survival. The chaos that ensued was a blur of calculated movements and primal instincts, the metallic tang of blood a stark contrast to my impassive demeanor.

Her brother, once a formidable force of retribution, now lay lifeless at my feet—a casualty in the silent war of survival I waged within myself. The aftermath was a symphony of disbelief and detachment, the echoes of my actions reverberating through the empty chambers of my soul.

Yet, amidst the wreckage of shattered lives and broken illusions, I remained unmoved, a stoic sentinel in a world consumed by chaos. The crimson stains of regret painted a haunting tableau on the canvas of my existence, a stark reminder of the darkness that dwelled within.

Now, back within the sterile confines of my prison cell, I am a ghostly figure haunted by the specter of that fateful encounter. The walls bear silent witness to the dance of death I orchestrated, a macabre performance in the theater of my mind.

And yet, amidst the silence and emptiness that envelops me, there lingers a perverse sense of satisfaction—a cold, detached acknowledgment of the power I wielded in a world governed by primal instincts and unyielding survival.

SEVEN
The Interview

And that's how I ended up here, sharing my life story with you.

Is it to your liking?

I've yet to find the perfect ring to encapsulate it all.

Contact the Author

Email: myviewoflifeonearth@gmail.com
Instagram: Patient_eye

www.ingramcontent.com/pod-product-compliance
Lightning Source LLC
LaVergne TN
LVHW021146160826
845679LV00023B/2064
9798893225273